D1269554

HISTORY'S KID
HEROES

THE UNDERGROUND RAILROAD ADVENTURE OF ALLEN JAY,

ANTISLAVERY ACTIVIST

BY **MARLENE TARG BRILL**
ADAPTED BY **EMMA CARLSON BERNE**
ILLUSTRATED BY **TED HAMMOND** AND **RICHARD PIMENTEL CARBAJAL**

Graphic Universe™ • Minneapolis • New York

INTRODUCTION

ALLEN JAY AND HIS FAMILY LIVED IN RANDOLPH, OHIO, DURING THE 1840S. THE JAYS BELONGED TO A RELIGIOUS GROUP CALLED THE SOCIETY OF FRIENDS, OR QUAKERS. QUAKERS BELIEVED EVERYONE—WHETHER WHITE OR BLACK—WAS EQUAL. QUAKERS DRESSED ALIKE IN PLAIN CLOTHES AND CALLED EVERYBODY "THEE," WHETHER STRANGER OR FRIEND.

MOST WHITE PEOPLE IN THE SOUTHERN UNITED STATES DID NOT TREAT AFRICAN AMERICANS AS EQUALS. THEY KEPT AFRICAN AMERICANS AS SLAVES. SLAVES WORKED ALL DAY WITHOUT PAY. ANY SLAVES WHO ESCAPED WERE HUNTED AND PUNISHED. PEOPLE WHO HELPED SLAVES ESCAPE WERE PUNISHED TOO.

ALLEN'S PARENTS, ISAAC AND RHODA JAY, HELPED SLAVES RUN AWAY EVEN THOUGH IT WAS DANGEROUS. THE JAYS WERE PART OF A SECRET GROUP CALLED THE UNDERGROUND RAILROAD.

PEOPLE WHO WORKED WITH THE UNDERGROUND RAILROAD HID RUNAWAY SLAVES IN BARNS, ATTICS, AND HIDDEN ROOMS. THEY GUIDED THE RUNAWAYS FROM ONE SAFE PLACE TO THE NEXT. RUNAWAYS TRAVELED BY FOOT, IN WAGONS, OR ON HORSEBACK, FOLLOWING SECRET ROUTES TO CANADA. THERE, EVERYONE WAS TREATED EQUALLY UNDER THE LAW. THE JAYS WERE CAREFUL NOT TO TELL OTHERS EXACTLY WHAT THEY DID —NOT EVEN THEIR CHILDREN. ELEVEN-YEAR-OLD ALLEN KNEW THAT HIS PARENTS FED AND HID STRANGERS WHO APPEARED AND DISAPPEARED MYSTERIOUSLY. BUT HE DIDN'T UNDERSTAND MUCH ABOUT SLAVERY— UNTIL THE DAY HE CAME FACE-TO-FACE WITH A RUNAWAY.

ALLEN REMEMBERED STORIES ABOUT OTHER FRIENDS WHO HELPED RUNAWAYS.

SOME FRIENDS HAD BEEN BEATEN. OTHERS HAD HAD THEIR HOMES BURNED.

ALLEN, THEE MAY SOON SEE A DARK-SKINNED MAN.

TAKE HIM INTO THE CORNFIELD TO HIDE HIM.

I MUST HURRY. HENRY WILL BE STARVING.

click!

HENRY! IT'S ME. DON'T SHOOT!

YOU GIVE ME A SCARE.

14

ALLEN HAD NEVER TRAVELED ALONE THROUGH THE WOODS IN THE DARK BEFORE. BEARS, WILDCATS, AND SNAKES ROAMED THE AREA. NOW SLAVE HUNTERS MIGHT BE LURKING IN THE WOODS TOO. BUT ALLEN KNEW WHAT HIS FATHER WANTED HIM TO DO.

IT'S ALLEN. WE MUST HURRY.

I'M GLAD TO SEE YOU, MASTER ALLEN. I BETTER HIDE DOWN ON THE BOTTOM OF THE BUGGY.

THERE'S ROOM DOWN HERE BY MY FEET.

A BIT TIGHT, BUT I CAN MANAGE.

AFTERWORD

ALLEN JAY GREW UP TO BECOME A WELL-KNOWN QUAKER MINISTER AND TEACHER. HE ALSO BECAME A FAMOUS SPEAKER, AND THIS AMAZED MANY PEOPLE. ALLEN WAS BORN WITH A HOLE IN THE ROOF OF HIS MOUTH THAT MADE HIM HARD TO UNDERSTAND SOMETIMES. BUT HIS POWERFUL WORDS OF PEACE AND LOVE WERE TREASURED BY MANY FRIENDS. AS AN OLDER MAN, ALLEN WROTE THE STORY OF HIS LIFE AND OF HIS MEETING WITH THE RUNAWAY SLAVE.

THE UNDERGROUND RAILROAD CONTINUED TO HELP PEOPLE UNTIL AFTER THE CIVIL WAR (1861-1865). THIS WAR BETWEEN THE STATES HELPED END SLAVERY IN AMERICA. BY THEN, MORE THAN 60,000 RUNAWAY SLAVES HAD PASSED TO FREEDOM THROUGH THE RAILROAD. YOUNG ALLEN JAY AND OTHER RAILROAD CONDUCTORS HELPED END ONE OF THE CRUELEST PRACTICES IN U.S. HISTORY.

FURTHER READING AND WEBSITES

EVANS, SHANE W. *UNDERGROUND*. NEW YORK: ROARING BROOK PRESS, 2011.

HUEY, LOIS MINER. *AMERICAN ARCHAEOLOGY UNCOVERS THE UNDERGROUND RAILROAD*. TARRYTOWN, NY: MARSHALL CAVENDISH, 2009.

KAMMA, ANNA. *IF YOU LIVED WHEN THERE WAS SLAVERY IN AMERICA*. NEW YORK: SCHOLASTIC, 2004.

MOORE, CATHY. *ELLEN CRAFT'S ESCAPE FROM SLAVERY*. MINNEAPOLIS: MILLBROOK PRESS, 2011.

NELSON, VAUNDA MICHEAUX. *ALMOST TO FREEDOM*. MINNEAPOLIS: CAROLRHODA BOOKS, 2003.

RAPPAPORT, DOREEN. *FREEDOM RIVER*. NEW YORK: HYPERION, 2007.

THE UNDERGROUND RAILROAD
HTTP://WWW.NATIONALGEOGRAPHIC.COM/FEATURES/99/RAILROAD/

UNDERSTANDING SLAVERY
HTTP://SCHOOL.DISCOVERYEDUCATION.COM/SCHOOLADVENTURES/SLAVERY/

WALDMAN, NEIL. *A LAND OF BIG DREAMERS: VOICES OF COURAGE IN AMERICA*. MINNEAPOLIS: MILLBROOK PRESS, 2011.

WAXMAN, LAURA HAMILTON. *HOW DID SLAVES FIND A ROUTE TO FREEDOM?: AND OTHER QUESTIONS ABOUT THE UNDERGROUND RAILROAD*. MINNEAPOLIS: LERNER PUBLICATIONS COMPANY, 2011.

WEIDT, MARYANN N. *HARRIET TUBMAN*. MINNEAPOLIS: LERNER PUBLICATIONS COMPANY, 2003.

WYETH, SHARON DENNIS. *FREEDOM'S WINGS: COREY'S UNDERGROUND RAILROAD DIARY*. NEW YORK: SCHOLASTIC PRESS, 2002.

ABOUT THE AUTHOR

MARLENE TARG BRILL HAS WRITTEN A NUMBER OF TITLES FOR LERNER PUBLISHING GROUP, UNDER ITS LERNER, MILLBROOK, AND TWENTY-FIRST CENTURY IMPRINTS. SHE LIVES IN WILMETTE, ILLINOIS.

ABOUT THE ADAPTER

EMMA CARLSON BERNE HAS WRITTEN AND EDITED MORE THAN TWO DOZEN BOOKS FOR YOUNG PEOPLE, INCLUDING BIOGRAPHIES OF SUCH DIVERSE FIGURES AS CHRISTOPHER COLUMBUS, WILLIAM SHAKESPEARE, THE HILTON SISTERS, AND SNOOP DOGG. SHE HOLDS A MASTER'S DEGREE IN COMPOSITION AND RHETORIC FROM MIAMI UNIVERSITY. MS. BERNE LIVES IN CINCINNATI, OHIO, WITH HER HUSBAND AND SON.

ABOUT THE ILLUSTRATORS

TED HAMMOND IS A CANADIAN ARTIST, LIVING AND WORKING JUST OUTSIDE OF TORONTO. HAMMOND HAS CREATED ARTWORK FOR EVERYTHING FROM FANTASY AND COMIC-BOOK ART TO CHILDREN'S MAGAZINES, POSTERS, AND BOOK ILLUSTRATION.

RICHARD PIMENTEL CARBAJAL HAS A BROAD SPECTRUM OF ILLUSTRATIVE SPECIALTIES. HIS BACKGROUND HAS FOCUSED ON LARGE-SCALE INSTALLATIONS AND SCENERY. CARBAJAL RECENTLY HAS EXPANDED INTO THE BOOK PUBLISHING AND ADVERTISING MARKETS.

Text copyright © 2012 by Marlene Targ Brill
Illustrations © 2012 by Lerner Publishing Group, Inc.

Graphic Universe™ is a trademark of Lerner Publishing Group, Inc.

Graphic Universe™
A division of Lerner Publishing Group, Inc.
241 First Avenue North
Minneapolis, MN 55401 U.S.A.

Website address: www.lernerbooks.com

Brill, Marlene Targ.
    The Underground Railroad adventure of Allen Jay, antislavery activist / by Marlene Targ Brill ; adapted by Emma Carlson Berne ; illustrated by Ted Hammond and Richard Pimentel Carbajal.
        p.   cm. — (History's kid heroes)
    Summary: Recounts in graphic novel format how Allen Jay, a young Quaker boy living in Ohio during the 1840s, helped a fleeing slave escape his master and make it to freedom through the Underground Railroad.
    Includes bibliographical references.
    ISBN: 978-0-7613-7804-4 (lib. bdg. : alk. paper)
    1. Graphic novels. [1. Graphic novels. 2. Underground Railroad—Fiction. 3. Fugitive slaves—Fiction. 4. Jay, Allen—Fiction. 5. Quakers—Fiction. 6. Brill, Marlene Targ. Allen Jay and the Underground Railroad—Adaptations.] I. Berne, Emma Carlson. II. Hammond, Ted, ill. III. Carbajal, Richard, ill. IV. Title.
PZ7.7.B75Un 2012
741.5'973—dc22   2011004745

Manufactured in the United States of America
1—MG—7/15/11